MORE HAUNTED HOUSE STORIES

by
EVE MARAR

kidsbooks
Incorporated

For my three free spirits:
Maya, Pia, and Devan

Contents

MORE
HAUNTED
HOUSE
STORIES

The Girl
in the Attic

The girl was always there. Marianne would stare up at the attic window, squinting her eyes against the glare of the sun. The pale girl with long blond hair would look down at her and wave. Marianne would smile and wave back.

Marianne had been unable to make out the girl's features clearly. The attic was on the third floor of the house. The cracked and dirty glass of the arched wood-frame window was thick and wavy, distorting her image. It was a sad face, though. Not once had Marianne seen her smile.

She had guessed her to be eleven or twelve, about the same age as herself. Each day, since first seeing the girl five days earlier, Marianne had crossed through the tall grass of the meadow with her dog, Spot, and approached the back of the house. The girl had waved each time she had seen Marianne, but she had never come down.

Marianne had been tempted to knock on the door. But the run-down Victorian farmhouse was so large and forbidding that, in truth, she lacked the courage.

If she hadn't seen the girl, she would have thought the house was empty. Whoever lived there certainly wasn't taking care of the place.

The paint, which was peeling off the sides of the house, was all blackened. Ivy had climbed up to the attic window threatening to cover it completely. The large rose bed was a mess. The roses had been allowed to grow as they pleased and had already reached the second floor of the house, entangled in a wild confusion of color. Ripe red strawberries, and plentiful loganberries now climbing crazily over the picket fence, had been left for the birds. Marianne knew that if she lived there, they wouldn't go to waste.

Marianne's family had only just moved to the small town of Knotsville, Maine. It was June. School wasn't due to start until September, and she didn't know a single soul. Her father was busy setting up his law practice and her mother was occupied with trying to find a house for them to live in.

It was going to be a long, lonely summer. Surely the girl—Alice she had decided to call her for now—must be lonely, too. She looked sad enough. *Yes,* Marianne had thought, *Alice suits her perfectly. Alice through the looking glass.*

Even Spot had found a friend. A large German shepherd, probably the girl's, kept watch from the back porch each day. The first day he had seen the dog, Spot had acted strangely. His hackles had sprung up, and a long, low growl had rumbled from his throat. He had barked furiously and had run off into the meadow, the tall grass hiding him from view. His persistent barking and Marianne's yells for him to come back had seemingly fallen on deaf ears. No one had come out of the house to find out who, or what, was causing all the commotion.

A short while later Spot had returned at

full speed, sliding to a halt just in front of Marianne. Repeatedly he had run off and returned, nudging her legs with his cold nose each time he came back, as though begging her to follow him.

The other dog's behavior had been just as strange. He hadn't moved from the back porch. He had pretended disinterest, staring at them with large mournful eyes, but Marianne had seen his bushy, brown tail wagging slowly. *Strange,* she had thought, *an unhappy-looking dog, and a sad-looking mistress.*

On the second day, Spot had been braver. He pushed open the rickety back gate and ventured a short way down the gravel walkway. Suddenly the other dog moved. He stood at the edge of the porch, watching, and let out a low whimper. Spot hesitated for only a split second before turning and charging back through the gate, disappearing into the meadow. Startled, Marianne had run after him.

"I can't blame you, boy," she'd said later, patting his head. "I don't even have the courage to knock on the door. There's something very strange about that house, Spot."

She couldn't get the girl or the dog out of her mind. She had lain sleepless for hours thinking about them. Finally, when sleep came, they were always in her dreams, watching and waiting. For what, though? Why didn't the girl come down to talk to her? Why didn't the dog come out to play with Spot?

The house, the dog, and the girl were Marianne's secret. She had decided that if Alice hadn't come down to talk to her by Friday, she would ask her father to take her over to the house. She was determined to have the mystery solved before the week was over.

Marianne felt compelled to return to the house each day. Spot seemed determined to befriend the German shepherd. On the third day he was brave enough to go up onto the porch. Marianne had held her breath, fearful of what might have happened next.

The dogs, eyeing each other warily, sniffed each other. The German shepherd barked softly and lifted a front paw in acceptance. Spot layed down by his side like an old friend. From where she stood, on the other side of the fence, Marianne sighed with relief at the thumping of happy tails.

Then she started up the walkway, but she stopped. Her change of mind was due to nothing more than fear. Perhaps the following day would bring the courage she needed to knock on the door.

Well, it had been five days, and the situation had barely altered. She still lacked the courage to knock on the door; the girl hadn't come down; and the dog never set foot off the porch. The only thing that had changed was that the dogs had become friends. How she wished the same for herself and the girl in the attic.

It was Friday. Marianne planned to tell her parents her secret that evening. She would ask one of them to go with her to the house over the weekend. As it turned out, her plans didn't work out quite as she'd expected.

"Don't wander off in the morning, Marianne. We're going to look at a house," her mother said excitedly. "It's going to need a lot of fixing up, as it's been empty for years, but the realtor thinks it's just what we're looking for."

"Where is it, Mom? What's it like?" asked Marianne.

"You'll see in the morning. I want to surprise you," said her mother. "You're going to love it, though."

Marianne decided her secret could wait one more day.

The following morning, as Mrs. Swan, the elderly realtor, turned into Appletree Lane, Marianne knew where they were going. She suddenly felt cold . . . very cold, as the station wagon stopped outside the front of the house . . . Alice's house.

"Surprise, Marianne. This is it. Magnificent, isn't it? Or at least it will be after we fix it up. Come on," said her mother eagerly as she opened the passenger door. "Let's look inside."

It's a surprise, all right, thought a confused Marianne. *Mrs. Swan's mistaken. How can the house be empty? Alice lives here.*

As Mrs. Swan struggled with the rusted padlock on the front door, Marianne's mother exclaimed, "Now, where's that dog of yours running off to?"

Marianne knew the answer to that. He'd gone to join his friend on the back porch. *Strange . . . the dog didn't bark when he heard us,* she thought. *But then, none of this makes any sense at all.*

The front door groaned open, and the light of day revealed a long narrow hall. Cobwebs hung from the chandelier and ran along the tops of the high walls. As they entered the house their footprints left an eerie trail on the dust-covered hardwood floor.

"Of course, the electricity's off," said Mrs. Swan. "That's why I brought along flashlights," she added, groping around in her tote bag. "Let's open some drapes and shutters and let some sunlight in."

She walked through a wide opening that led into a large living room. Marianne's parents followed. Marianne stayed back, her eyes fixed on the wooden staircase at the end of the long hallway. She knew these were the stairs that led up to the attic . . . and Alice.

Marianne shivered. She was scared. She wanted to run and join her parents, but something . . . someone . . . was pulling her toward the stairs. As though being drawn by a giant magnet, she seemed no longer to be in control of her own actions. Gripping the wooden banister tightly, Marianne slowly began to climb the stairs.

The landing led to a long narrow corridor. It was dark upstairs. Grateful for the flashlight, Marianne beamed it down the corridor. Like the hallway downstairs, doors led off on either side. *Which is* her *room?* she wondered nervously. She shone the light directly ahead. Marianne screamed. She screamed at the top of her lungs.

Heavy footsteps pounded on the stairs behind her. "What's the matter?" her father asked in alarm. "Are you okay?"

"D-Dad!" she stuttered, clutching tightly to his arm. "Th-there's s-someone at the end of the c-corridor ... someone walking t-toward me."

"Marianne! Your imagination's playing tricks on you," he assured her. "I must admit, though, it is a little spooky up here in the dark, but there's no one here."

He shone his flashlight in front of them. Suddenly he chuckled loudly. "Marianne, there's your answer ... a full-length mirror at the end of the corridor. You were watching yourself."

Still laughing, he put a comforting arm around his daughter's shoulders. She was still trembling. "Apparently there's a girl's room up here, with all her things in it. Mrs. Swan was about to tell us the story behind it when you screamed. You gave us quite a scare, young lady, let me tell you.

"Let's find her room and let in some light. Perhaps you'll find something there to amuse yourself," he added.

Marianne, clinging to her father's arm, followed him as he began to open the doors along the corridor. "Ah, here it is," he said as he beamed his light into the second room on the right. Walking over to the window, he pulled up the pink shade.

It was a young girl's bedroom, all right. On top of the pink bedspread on a white canopy bed, dolls and stuffed animals were propped neatly against two ruffled pink pillows. Like everything else, the books stacked neatly on shelves behind the bed were covered with dust.

"I wonder why all these things were left here?" her father mused. "Normally people take their possessions with them when they move, especially a child."

Because the child's still here, Dad, Marianne wanted to tell him, but the words wouldn't come out of her mouth.

"You're as white as a ghost, Marianne. Come back down with me and listen to Mrs. Swan's story. It must be quite some tale," said her father.

"You go ahead, Dad," she said softly. "I'll be okay." *Who am I trying to convince?* she asked herself. *I've never been so scared in my life.*

Her father gave her a quick hug. "Be

careful. Mrs. Swan said to stay away from the attic. It's not safe up there."

As he left the room and headed back down the corridor, he called out, "Sure you don't want to join us?"

She was about to change her mind, about to run after him, when her eyes caught the gaze of a girl in a photo. Marianne froze.

It was the girl in the attic, kneeling by the side of a dog, a German shepherd, staring back at her. The girl's eyes commanded her to stay. It was the same girl and the same dog, yet they were different. The girl was smiling. The dog looked happy.

Suddenly Marianne's feet were taking her down the corridor. *How did I get here?* she wondered in bewilderment. *I don't remember leaving the room.* As though watching herself in a dream, she found herself heading back toward the mirror.

Standing in front of it, she could see it was attached to a door. The door, once white, was now gray and peeling, marred by dark brown patches. Marianne needed no one to tell her that the damage done to the back of the door

20

had been caused by fire. Most of the paint had been burnt off, leaving the door scorched and blackened. She watched in a daze as her hand, a hand with a mind of its own, moved to the doorknob. It turned the knob and the door pulled open.

Marianne was drawn onto another landing. A large skylight above showed two flights of stairs. One led down to a lower level, and the other one led up above. In the beam of her flashlight she could see a door that was as charred as the one she'd just opened. This door had to lead to the attic, where the mystery would be solved. That is, if she could find enough courage to climb the steps and open the door.

Her father's warning flashed through her mind. *Stay away from the attic, Marianne. It's not safe.* How could she explain that it wasn't her decision to make . . . that someone else was making it for her?

With no regard as to whether the fire-damaged stairs would give way under her weight, she began to climb, holding on to a charred wall for support. There were eight steps. Each one she took brought her closer and closer to the attic.

A wooden bar had slipped down into its catch, blocking the door from the outside. Marianne's hand was drawn to the bar. Slowly she lifted it up. She turned the doorknob and pushed the door open.

Trembling, she leaned against the door frame as she shone her flashlight into the semidarkness. Immediately facing her, framed against the light of the window, was the girl in the photo, in the same pink dress.

She smiled at Marianne. "I knew you'd come," she whispered. "The bar slipped down. It does that sometimes, you know. I couldn't open the door. Thanks."

Goose bumps sprang up on Marianne's arms and neck as the girl seemed to float toward her, drawing with her the light from the window. A thin cold hand reached out and touched Marianne's arm, sending chills down her spine. "I've waited so long for you to come," said the girl.

Then she ran past Marianne, pulling her out onto the landing. "Come on. Let's go outside," she said. "I can't wait to see Toby. I know he's waiting for me."

She flew down the stairs, dragging a terrified Marianne behind her. In an instant they were in a small room that would have been in total darkness had it not been for the strange light coming from the girl.

She flung open the door, which led into the kitchen. Skipping across the floor, the girl was out on the back porch in no time at all. "Toby! Toby! It's me, boy. It's me!" she cried.

Marianne got outside just in time to see the dog leap up, knocking the girl to the ground. As they romped and wrestled, the girl laughed and cried at the same time. Toby barked, his tail swishing with sheer joy.

Marianne had been too dazed, too overwhelmed to speak, until then. "Who are you?" she whispered. "What were you doing in the attic?"

The girl looked up at Marianne. "I told you. I've been locked in for a long time. We've waited so long. We don't know how to thank you," she said.

THE GIRL IN THE ATTIC

As though he had understood his mistress, Toby ran to Marianne and jumped up and licked her face. With a final bark and glance at Spot, he ran to the girl's side.

Before Marianne could speak, the girl and the dog were running down the gravel walkway and out through the back gate. "Wait!" she called. "Will I see you again? What's your name?"

The girl stopped and, turning to look at her, called back, "Alicia. My name's Alicia. I don't know if we'll be back. Good-bye."

With a parting wave, she ran through the meadow. Marianne heard the dog bark for the last time. Then the girl and her dog vanished as though they had never existed.

Startled by a loud noise behind her, Marianne whirled around. Her mother was clearly upset. "Didn't you hear us calling you? We were scared half to death when we realized you'd been up in the attic. What possessed you to go up there after you'd been warned not to? And how on earth did you get out here without us seeing you?" she asked.

"Alicia brought me down the back stairs," said Marianne.

Her mother gasped. Mrs. Swan, standing behind her, paled visibly.

"Did you say Alicia, Marianne?" asked her mother, her voice quivering unsteadily. "If this is your idea of a joke, then I don't think it's very funny." She looked questioningly at Marianne. "You heard Mrs. Swan's story, didn't you? Then you thought you'd play this awful joke on us," she said.

"Mom," protested Marianne, "you know me better than that. You know I wouldn't have disobeyed you. Alicia made me go up and let her out. She's been making me come to the house all week. I meant to tell you about her last night.

"It's all so confusing. How long has she been in the attic? Who takes care of her?" asked Marianne.

Mrs. Swan glanced at Marianne's mother and sank down onto the old bench near the back door. "Fifteen years ago, Marianne, there was a fire in the house," she said. "Mrs.

Martin, Alicia's mother, was in the yard when she smelled the smoke. She tried to get into the house, but she had locked herself out. She called for Alicia, but there was no answer. Thinking Alicia had gone off to play with her dog, Mrs. Martin drove off in her car to call the fire department.

"When the firemen arrived, the dog was dead on the porch. He'd died trying to break down the door to get to Alicia. They found her later in the attic, dead from smoke inhalation. The bar had slipped down, locking her in.

"Mrs. Martin never forgave herself. She and her husband moved away. She insisted on leaving Alicia's things behind. She refused to accept the fact that her daughter was dead.

"Mrs. Martin died recently, and her husband decided to sell the house. It's never been offered for sale before. His wife would never allow it. She said it was Alicia's home."

Mrs. Swan was conscious of the pink photo frame she was clutching in her hand. She had been holding it when Marianne's father had discovered that the door leading to the attic was open. She held it out for Marianne to see. "Is this the girl you saw, Marianne?" she asked.

Marianne gasped. Her mother stared at it in disbelief. The frame was empty. The photo was gone!

Marianne's father, who had been listening from the doorway, walked out onto the porch and stared at the empty frame for a while. Then he walked over to Marianne and her mother. Placing his arms around their shoulders, he said shakily, "I'm sorry, Mrs. Swan, but we won't be taking the house after all."

Soldier on the Beach

Despite the pounding of the waves against the rocks, the wind that whipped against the sea, and the distance, he sensed her presence.

He had been staring out to sea when she first saw him. Perhaps he was watching the old fishing trawler heading back to Lowestoft Harbor with its catch of herring or mackerel. He turned now to look in her direction. Their eyes met. He smiled, a warm, toothless smile.

He was dressed in a strange army uniform, yet he looked far too old to be a soldier. White hair stuck out from under his khaki cap. His face, lined and weather-beaten, looked kind, yet had a sternness about it that implied toughness if the situation demanded it. Three V-shaped yellow stripes on the left sleeve of his khaki jacket indicated that he must be an officer.

Kate's aunt Mildred had told her tales of some of the strange village people. Without a doubt, this man had to be one of them.

He looked interesting . . . looked as though he would be fun to talk to, yet she was sensible enough not to take any chances. Kate glanced around. There was no one on the beach except the old soldier.

She stared down at him from the relative safety of the cliffside. She couldn't help but wonder what he was doing all alone on the small isolated beach and how he could have managed the steep climb down to it.

She might have passed that way every day during the summer and never have discovered the overgrown path that zigzagged down the cliff. However, she had seen a rabbit dart through the heather at the top of the cliff and had followed it, stumbling upon the path worn into the cliffside.

For want of anything better to do, she had followed the path's zigzagging line down the steep slope, and she had thought it her secret . . . until she saw him.

The beach was separated from the other

beaches by huge boulders. Kate assumed the only access was from the cliffside itself.

Kate waved and turned to climb back up. As she turned she hesitated for just a moment. Had she imagined she had seen a glimmer of relief flash across his face? It was just then that she noticed he was sitting on an old wooden box. Written on the side in bold red letters was the word *Ammunition.*

He was there again the next day, staring out to sea. It seemed as though he had not moved from one day to the next. It was almost as though he were watching and waiting for someone . . . or something. It looked as though the beach was his own private property . . . that perhaps he was guarding it against intruders.

Kate shuddered as he turned to look up at her. It was uncanny the way he always seemed to know she was there. She was tempted to go down to talk to him, but something held her back. What was it? Fear? She wasn't sure. Whatever it was, he showed no signs of welcoming her company.

On the third day she approached the beach

again. Somehow she found the courage to go farther down the path than she had dared before. Kate hoped he would speak to her . . . encourage her to join him. But the chilling look in his steel-gray eyes stopped her in her tracks. They seemed to flash a warning signal. He frowned and shook his head slowly. His cold, unwelcoming expression sent shivers down her spine.

Kate turned and fled back up the path. Trembling, her legs scratched and bleeding from running through the prickly bushes, she looked down from the safety of the cliff top. The beach was deserted. The old soldier was nowhere in sight.

Her aunt Mildred was just putting lunch on the table when Kate burst into the kitchen. Mildred Wilkins looked at her niece in alarm. "Whatever's the matter, Kate? Are you all right? Goodness! What happened to your legs?" she asked.

"I'm okay," Kate said breathlessly, "really I am. I just had a bit of a scare, that's all."

"By the looks of you, it was more than just

a bit. Come and sit down. You can tell me about it while I clean those scratches. I'll just go and get the antiseptic," said Aunt Mildred.

When her aunt returned to the kitchen, Kate said, "Aunt Mildred, remember you told me the village is full of strange characters? Who's the elderly man who dresses in an army uniform?"

Her aunt looked puzzled. "I know just about everyone in the village, Kate, and they all know me. Why, I only have to sneeze twice and at least half a dozen people will call to find out if I have a cold. I can't think of anyone around here like that. Why do you ask?"

"I've seen him down on the beach. I've seen him for the past three days now, always in the same place. I'd just found enough courage to go down to talk to him when he scared me away. He didn't say a word . . . didn't do anything, really. It was the look on his face that frightened me. I was so scared I ran all the way home," Kate explained.

"Well, you should know better than to talk to strangers anyway, Kate. I wonder who he is though," said Aunt Mildred.

"Will you come to the beach with me this afternoon?" asked Kate. "I'd like you to see him for yourself."

"We can't this afternoon, Kate. I'm taking you into Norwich to meet some more of your relatives. They're all eager to get to know you. Your cousin Julie wants to take you shopping, and I want you to see the castle and the cathedral. We'll go tomorrow. You've made me really curious," said Aunt Mildred.

That night, during a dinner of fish and chips, Mildred Wilkins said thoughtfully, "It's strange you should ask me about an old soldier. All afternoon, for some reason, I've been thinking about your great-grandfather. He was a professional soldier, you know. He served for a long time in India. He had a voice like a foghorn . . . loud enough to awaken the dead.

"He was so disappointed when he was told he was too old to serve in the Second World War. He knew this area like the back of his hand, though, and was given the rank of sergeant major in the Home Guard. He would patrol the beaches looking for German planes or ships threatening to attack our shoreline.

"After dinner, I'll get out the family album and show you some pictures. I might even have a spare one you can take back to America as a remembrance of your British heritage. It'll be like a family heirloom, so you must promise to take good care of it."

After the dinner dishes had been cleared, Mildred Wilkins crossed over to the bookcase, opened the glass doors, and took down a faded leather photo album.

"Ah, yes. Here he is," said Aunt Mildred. "Kate, let me introduce you to Sergeant Major Walter Wilkins of the First East Anglian Regiment. He died an awful death, you know, in 1943, the same year your father was born. . . ."

Mildred Wilkins' voice trailed off as she saw the stunned look on her niece's face. "Kate, what is it? What's wrong?" she asked.

It was a while before Kate could answer. "You don't have to introduce us. We've already met. I know you're going to think I'm crazy, but that's the man on the beach. I'd recognize him anywhere."

Mildred Wilkins shook her head and smiled. "Your imagination's running wild, Kate. That's not possible, though I must admit it's strange . . . a strange coincidence, I mean. I was just about to tell you how your great-grandfather died.

"During the Second World War land mines were placed in certain places along the beaches, just in case the enemy, the Germans, tried to invade England by sea. Your great-grandfather may have been too old for active duty, but he had all his wits about him. His eyesight and hearing were as keen as any young soldier's.

"Anyway, his job as sergeant in the Home Guard was to patrol the beaches. No one knew how or why it happened, but one day he stepped on one of the land mines. He was killed on the very same beach he had sworn to guard with his life."

Kate ran her finger over the face of the old soldier. In a strangely hushed voice she asked, "Did it happen on a tiny isolated stretch of beach, cut off from the main beach by large rocks? Did it happen at Benicha Point?"

It was Aunt Mildred's turn to look stunned. "Good heavens. That's exactly where it did happen. Not too many folks even know of that beach's existence," she said.

"Well, that's where I saw him. For the past three days he's been sitting in his uniform on that beach, on an old ammunition box. Will you come with me in the morning? I don't expect you to believe me until you see him with your own eyes," Kate said.

Then she looked thoughtfully at her aunt. "I don't know if you'll be able to make the climb down the cliff. It's pretty steep. I think it's the only way down. I wonder how he manages it."

"Wild horses couldn't keep me away, Kate. I want answers. I need to see for myself," said Aunt Mildred. "Don't you worry, either, about my being able to make it, young lady. I may be fifteen years older than your father, but there's plenty of life in this old dog yet. I do walk five miles every day, you know."

The next morning Kate found her aunt at the kitchen table, staring at the local newspaper. Mildred Wilkins's normally rosy cheeks were unusually pale. Her hands shook as she held the paper. Kate glanced over her aunt's shoulder. She gasped as she read the headline: "Climber Killed By Old Land Mine."

Kate sat down and took the paper from her aunt's trembling hands. In a shaky voice she read, "Fifty-year-old James Kent died yesterday in a freak accident. He was killed when stepping on a land mine that had been planted over forty years ago at Benicha Point. A police spokesman said no one is certain why the mine had not been discovered before. One possible explanation is that the beach is quite inaccessible, and most people are unaware of its existence.

"Mr. Kent, an avid climber, had climbed down the cliff to the isolated beach. Residents reported the sound of a loud explosion around 7:00 P.M. last evening.

"The beach has been closed off to the public until further notice."

Kate's long summer vacation in England was almost over. Many weeks had passed since the accident on the beach. She was due to return to the United States the following weekend.

"Aunt Mildred, I want to have one last look at the beach before I go back home. I want to go down to the beach and look around. I heard on the news last night that it's just been declared safe," said Kate.

Kate's aunt agreed they could go that day.

Hand in hand Kate and her aunt walked over the smooth sand of the deserted beach. Neither spoke as they noticed an impression in the sand of two large footprints next to a rectangular indentation . . . one that could have been caused by an old ammunition box.

There was a cave at the base of the cliff. Nervously Kate entered, clutching tightly to her aunt's arm. Something shiny, wedged between two rocks, glimmered in the filtered sunlight. Kate bent down to pick it up.

It was an old brass button with the picture of a woman engraved on it. Aunt Mildred shook her head as she sat down on a large chunk of rock.

"Your great-grandfather wasn't allowed to wear his regimental uniform when he served in the Home Guard during the war. He had to wear the Home Guard uniform. He always carried one of his regimental buttons, though, for good luck. This button came off a uniform of the First East Anglian Regiment."

Mildred Wilkins sighed. "No one will ever believe this, Kate, but your great-grandfather, who died over forty years ago, saved your life this summer!"

A Ghost
of a Chance

"Jen, don't let go of my hand," Brian sobbed. The uncaring walls of the pitch-black cave echoed his crying like the sound of wailing ghosts. "It's all my s-stupid f-fault. I'm s-sorry."

Jennifer turned to wipe his tears. Fumbling for his face in the dark, she wasn't sure she had found her target. Her hands, numb from the chilling cold, shook violently. She was as terrified as her brother. She just didn't want him to know that.

"Don't worry, Brian. I'll get us out of here," she said with a confidence she didn't feel. Her voice bounced back at her from the unseen walls of the cave.

Jennifer never knew such darkness existed . . . that black could be so black. There was no flashlight as there had been during a recent power failure. There was no moon and no stars, and there were no flames from a campfire, to offer comfort as there had been at the Girl Scout weekend camp. They couldn't see one inch in front of them, and they were lost . . . completely lost.

"Don't take your watch, Jennifer," her mother had said. "You're bound to lose it, or get it wet." How long ago had that been? She had lost all track of time. Her watch wouldn't have done much good anyway. She couldn't have seen the hands. They wouldn't have shown her the way out, either.

"Thank g-goodness Mom made us wear jackets," Brian stuttered. "We'd be frozen without them."

"Not only that, our arms would be as raw as our legs. Do yours hurt as much as mine?" moaned Jennifer. "Why did we have to wear shorts today?"

Mom, can you read my mind? she pleaded silently. *We need help.*

Twelve-year-old Jennifer Meyers thought of all the times her mother had anticipated what she was about to say or do. "How did you know I was going to say that?" she'd ask in surprise. Her mother would smile and give her standard reply. "Because I'm your mother, that's why."

If there's such a thing as telepathy, Jennifer prayed silently, *let it work now. Mom! We need you! Come and find us!*

"Jen, can we sit for a while? My hands and legs hurt, and I'm tired. Please, let's rest for a few minutes," begged Brian.

Jennifer groped with her left hand. She gasped as something sharp poked her finger. She sucked the warm sticky blood as her foot bumped against the jagged edge of a rock.

She felt around carefully. "There's a ledge here," Jennifer said wearily. "We'll rest there . . . just for a minute."

They sat down, clutching each other tightly. They'd lost each other once. They didn't want it to happen again. "Feel for sharp pieces of rock before you lean back," she warned. "You might stab yourself."

Jennifer closed her eyes. She could see exactly as much as she could with them open. Nothing. Nothing but empty blackness.

Shivering from fear and cold, brother and sister huddled together for warmth and comfort. The sound of chattering teeth mocked them as the echoes mimicked their sound.

Despite the penetrating cold, Jennifer felt a sudden surge of warmth for her brother that she'd never really known before. She and Brian, three years her junior, were like night and day. They always seemed to be fighting. Lately she'd even begun to think she didn't like him much at all. *Why does it take something terrible like this to bring us closer together?*

Jennifer had stopped being angry with Brian hours ago . . . at least it had seemed like hours since they'd first set foot in the cave.

They had gone to the beach looking for shells. Brian wanted to enter a shell collection in the school's science fair. They'd been lucky. The tide was low. They found three sand dollars, two in perfect condition, and an assortment of shells, including a big abalone shell.

They'd spent a while at a tide pool, hunting for sand crabs and examining the star-fish. As usual, Brian had grown restless. Before Jennifer was aware of it, he'd disappeared out of sight around the corner of a steep cliff. "Jen, I've found a cave," he had yelled excitedly. "What fun. Let's explore."

She left the buckets and spades and ran in search of him. When she rounded the corner, Brian was nowhere in sight. At the base of the cliff a cave entrance gaped open like the mouth of a yawning giant.

"Brian Meyers, wait for me. You don't know what's in there. You could get hurt," she called out as she followed him into the mouth of the cave.

The entrance had been brightened by sunlight, but the back of the huge cave was dark and eerie. Brian had disappeared.

"Brian, where are you?" she yelled in alarm. The resounding echo of her voice startled her.

"Look down to your left, Jen. There's a small opening in the wall near the ground. Slide down through it. It's neat," he called back. Brian's voice sounded weird as it bounced around the cave.

"Don't take one more step, Brian. Don't move a muscle," she ordered. "People have been lost in caves, you know . . . and worse. I'm coming to get you."

She sought out the opening. *I'm sure I'm going to regret this,* she thought as she slid down a sandy slope. It's steepness alarmed her. She yelled as her knee grazed against a sharp rock.

"Wait till I get my hands on you, you . . . featherbrain. How are we going to climb back up?" Jennifer said.

The inner cave was very dark with only a thin shaft of light streaming in to offer comfort. Brian was nowhere in sight. "Come back right now, Brian," she yelled. "I'm scared. I don't like it in here."

"Hold on, Jen. I'm a bit lost. Yell. I'll follow your voice," Brian said. "I'd give anything for a flashlight."

"I'm so mad at you, Brian. Your punishment is having to listen to me sing." She covered her ears to block out the echoes as she sang. The walls accompanied her, just a few beats behind.

Suddenly a deafening scream filled the cave and interrupted Jennifer's singing. "Brian. Are you okay?" she yelled in panic. "What's wrong?"

"Something slimy just crawled over my foot," he cried. She could tell from his shaky voice that Brian was finding cave exploration far less fun than he had just a short while ago. "Jen, I hear you, but I can't find my way back.

"I'm scared, Jen. If we both yell, maybe we could meet each other halfway. Come and look for me. It's so dark and spooky. It stinks, too. Everything's slimy. Things are crawling everywhere!" he cried.

"You stay still, Brian. Keep talking. The crawling things are probably just cave salamanders. They won't hurt you," Jennifer said.

She had been scared, too. With her heart pounding and her thoughts racing, she entered another tunnel that was pitch-black. It had been low tide when they'd arrived at the beach. When was high tide? How far did the tide come in? From the kelp and seaweed she could feel in the cave, it was obvious that the sea would flood through. Even standing on tiptoe, Jennifer could not have reached above the waterline.

"Brian, don't panic," she yelled, trying to keep the fear out of her voice. "I'm coming to find you." It seemed like a long, long time before they found each other.

Jennifer was startled back to the present. Water lapped at her feet. Brian had fallen asleep. She woke him, trying to stay calm.

"We have to move, Brian. The tide's coming in. We have to climb upward," she said.

Numbly they struggled to their feet. Clutching on to each other, they groped blindly until they found a gap in the wall. "This way, Brian. Hurry," said Jennifer.

They seemed to be in the bowels of the earth, in a maze of tunnels connecting cave after cave that led seemingly nowhere. For all Jennifer knew, they could have been going around in circles. The water was now up to her ankles.

She had tried to stay calm, tried to be brave, but her fear was turning to panic. She had lost all hope of them finding their way out.

Suddenly her foot caught on a chunk of rock. She fell forward, dragging Brian with her. Jennifer lay on the cold wet ground and sobbed in despair.

A small hand fumbled and grasped her foot. Brian groped and found her head. Stroking her wet hair, he said, "It's all right, Jen. We'll find our way out. I'm sorry for getting you into this mess."

Jennifer sat up and put her arm around her brother's shoulder. She was cold, soaking wet, and terrified. *Mom, Dad, can you hear me? Beman, where are you, boy? I need you. Find us. Help us. Please!*

Jennifer thought longingly of her Labrador retriever, as coal-black as the caves themselves. If only her mother had let him come with them that morning.

"He's not feeling too well, Jennifer. If he's

no better by this afternoon, we'll take him to the vet," her mother had said. It was strange. She had wanted to stay with him, but her mother had insisted that they go to the beach. *Beman,* she prayed, *if only you were here, boy.*

If only they were back at the rented cottage, safe with Mom and Dad and Beman. They weren't, though. They were lost in a confusion of caves with water lapping menacingly at their feet.

Something wet and rough brushed against Jennifer's cheek. She sat bolt upright and screamed. Deafening echoes bounced back at her, scaring her even more. Brian grabbed her arm. Then there was a soft bark and the sound of panting and a tail thumping against the wall.

"Beman," whispered Jennifer in disbelief. "Is that you, boy?" A familiar lick and nuzzle of his head told her it was indeed her dog.

"You clever dog. You found us. I don't know how you did it, but you did. It's a miracle. You read my mind." Her tears of despair became tears of relief as she pressed her face thankfully against his. She wrapped her arms around his neck. "I love you, Beman. I've never been so happy to see anyone in my life. Help us find our way out, boy. Help us."

Beman barked and, gripping her sleeve between his teeth, urged her to follow him. She stood up and found his tail. With Brian clinging to the back of her jacket, they groped desperately in the darkness, trusting their lives to their dog.

They seemed to be going deeper and deeper underground. Water now lapped around Jennifer's knees. Unseen obstacles jabbed at them as they fumbled blindly at a snail's pace.

"Are you sure Beman knows what he's doing, Jen?" asked Brian. "The water's getting higher. I'm really scared."

"We have to trust him, Brian. We have no choice." Jennifer hoped he hadn't noticed the doubt in her voice.

Brian's hand was suddenly wrenched from Jennifer's jacket. There was a loud groan and a thump in the darkness behind her. She turned in alarm in the direction of the sound. "Jen, don't lose me," Brian moaned. "My foot's stuck. I can't move it. It hurts."

"Hang on, Brian, don't panic," called Jennifer, trying to stay calm. "Beman, find Brian, boy."

The dog turned and, with Jennifer still clinging to his tail, led her to Brian. He sighed with relief as she clutched his arm. "I'm going underwater to try and move your foot. Hold on," Jennifer said.

She groped her way down, and with a deep gasp and a splash, she was underwater. She fumbled and tugged in vain at his trapped foot.

Coughing and spitting as she surfaced, she gasped, "It's wedged between two rocks. I can't budge them. I'll go back under. I'll tug, and you pull as hard as you can. Maybe I can get your foot out of your sneaker."

A few more minutes of frantic struggling and Brian's foot was free but he screamed with pain.

"A-agh!" howled the walls. "A-agh!"

"Jen, I can't walk. My leg really hurts. The water's coming in fast. We're going to drown, I know it," Brian cried.

"Oh, no, we're not. We're going to get out of here. Put your arms around my neck. I'll carry you, piggyback style. Come on, Beman. Take us to safety," commanded Jennifer.

With Beman swimming in front, Jennifer clutched onto his tail with one hand, supporting Brian with the other. Brian felt their way with his free hand.

"Brian," she whispered, hardly daring to believe what was happening, "the water's going down. We're climbing up." There was hope after all. Beman's panting was becoming heavier and heavier.

Jennifer remembered the vet's warning. "He's getting old, Jennifer. His heart isn't as strong as it used to be. He has to start taking it easy."

"Slow down, boy. Take it easy. I think we're going to be all right," she said.

They struggled upward, farther and

farther away from the threatening water. Jennifer needed to rest but dared not. She didn't know how much longer she could carry Brian. There wasn't one bone in her body that didn't ache, one place she didn't hurt.

She reached down and felt Brian's ankle. The foot was turned at a strange angle. The swelling was worse. It might be broken. There was no way he could stand on that foot.

Brian jerked his head. For one frightening moment Jennifer lost her footing. "Stay still," she yelled. "You almost killed us both."

Brian wriggled excitedly on her back. "Sorry, Jen. Look up. I can see light. Tell me I'm not dreaming. We're going to be OK, aren't we?" he asked.

Jennifer stopped. "I'll put you down for a minute." She needed to rest. She was exhausted.

Brian slid off her back and sat against the wall on a platform of rock. "Jen! The rocks are dry. The water doesn't rise this high. We're safe!" he exclaimed.

Jennifer gasped with relief as she looked up. A welcoming shaft of light broke the darkness like a lazer beam cutting an opening for them through the cold hard rocks.

She squeezed her brother's shoulder. "I think we're going to be OK, but there's still a steep climb ahead. I'm not sure how much farther I can carry you. I'll get you as high as I can, and then I'll go for help. I'll send Beman back down to stay with you."

Jennifer kept her fears to herself. *What if the opening is too small for me to climb through? she thought. What if I can't climb that high? The walls are terribly steep.*

Jennifer knelt by her dog's side. She cradled his head in her arms. "You did it, boy. You did it. You saved our lives." His tail wagged furiously as he licked her cheek. "Poor you," she said in surprise. "I thought your coat would keep you warm. You feel really cold, too."

Where Jennifer got her strength from she would never know. She managed to carry Brian another ten feet or so up the rugged slope before setting him down on a wide ledge of rock. There was still a long, perilous climb ahead.

Glancing up, Jennifer winced from the sudden brightness. Above her, light and safety lay waiting. Below, terrifying darkness threatened to swallow them up. Had they really climbed out of such a hellish place?

Jennifer looked in concern at Brian. He was in a lot of pain. He needed help quickly.

"Don't move, Brian, and don't fall asleep," she instructed. "You might fall off the ledge. I'll be back with help as quickly as I can," she said.

With a reassuring tousle of Brian's soaking wet hair and an impulsive kiss on his forehead, Jennifer turned to make her upward climb. She could hear Brian shivering. With no regard for herself, she took off her jacket and turned and placed it over his shoulders. "Be back soon," she said as lightly as she could.

Slowly, painstakingly, Jennifer made her way upward, Beman guiding the way. Clawing, pulling, dragging, she worked her way toward the welcoming light.

All of a sudden Beman was out of sight. The beam of light had fanned out to light her way, the blackness replaced by an eerie gray that cast sinister shadows around her.

She looked up. Beman peered down at her, eyes wide, his familiar tongue hanging down, panting breathlessly. His blackness, framed against the clear blue sky, was the most beautiful sight she had ever seen.

The last few feet of the climb posed a terrifying challenge. Rocks gave way under her hands and feet, crumbling and tumbling down into the forbidding hole. Jennifer was terrified she would tumble down with them, or that Brian would be hit with some of the falling rocks. Each time she paused in fear and exhaustion, a gentle bark from above encouraged her onward and upward toward her goal.

Finally Jennifer reached up and pulled herself out of the cave. She felt the comforting softness of thick grass. A cool, gentle breeze swept over her hand. Something wet and rough brushed across her bloodied outstretched fingers.

Jennifer hoisted herself up. She was safe. She bent down and hugged her dog in gratitude and love. Tears of relief rolled down her grimy cheeks. Beman lifted his front paw and touched her face as though to wipe away her tears, just as she had done earlier for Brian. He whined softly.

With a start, Jennifer remembered Brian lying helpless so far down beneath them. She turned and yelled through the opening, "Brian! We made it. Can you hear me?"

"He . . . ar . . . m . . . e . . . ee!" answered the echoes from deep below.

"Brian! Brian!!" she screamed frantically. The only reply came from the unfriendly caves that had seemed so intent on trapping them forever.

Jennifer looked frantically around her. Even though her family had been on vacation in the area many times before, everything now looked strangely unfamiliar. She was high up on a cliff. Way down below, the sea pounded its white foam against the sides of the rocky cliffs. The beach had disappeared. So had Beman.

"Beman! Beman! Where are you, boy?" called Jennifer. There was no response. *That's strange,* she thought in alarm. *He always comes when I call. He must have gone back down to stay with Brian. I'm sure that's it. Right now I've got to find help for Brian.*

Jennifer ran across the clifftop as fast as her aching body would allow. What if Brian had been hit by falling rocks or knocked off the ledge? What if he panicked and tried to climb up himself? What if . . . ?

Her panicky thoughts were interrupted by the welcome sight of a police car parked on a dirt road at the top of the cliff. A police officer was scanning the area with binoculars. *This must be what a mirage looks like,* she thought with relief. Through cracked dry lips she screamed, "Help! Help!"

Her voice carried through the air on the gentle breeze. The young officer turned, waved his arm, and started to run toward her.

"You must be Jenny Meyers," he said, relief showing in his face. "There are a lot of people out searching for you and your brother."

"Brian's still down there in the cave. He's hurt," Jennifer told him breathlessly.

From then on things happened fast. Before she knew it, she had a blanket wrapped around her and the policeman was on the radio, calling for help. Then she grabbed his hand and ran with him to the cave opening.

"Brian," Jennifer yelled. "Hold on. Help's here." There was still no reply.

The quiet clifftop became a sudden hive of activity, swarming with police, fire fighters, and paramedics. Paramedics and a canvas stretcher were lowered into the cave. An anxious and relieved Mr. and Mrs. Meyers arrived just in time to see Brian being hoisted out of the cave, in pain but safe.

In an instant they were all in an ambulance, being rushed to the hospital, the blaring sirens breaking the stillness of the early evening.

Jennifer, lying snugly on the ambulance

bed, suddenly remembered their dog. She turned in alarm to look at Brian. "Brian, we forgot Beman. He didn't get left down in the cave, did he?" she asked.

Drowsily Brian turned his head to answer. He looked puzzled. "I thought he stayed with you. He didn't come back down to me," he said.

"He must have. He wasn't on the cliff. He disappeared a few seconds after I was safely out of the cave. He didn't even come when I called," she explained.

Jennifer glanced questioningly at her mother. Mrs. Meyer's face had paled, and she was staring at her daughter with a strange, bewildered expression. Jennifer looked up at her father. He had a similar puzzled look on his face.

"What do you mean Beman didn't come when you called? When did you last see him?" their mother asked.

"In the cave, Mom. Beman found us. He led us to safety. We'd have drowned without him. He saved our lives," said Jennifer.

Mrs. Meyers looked stunned. She sat

looking at Jennifer and Brian in shocked silence. Mr. Meyers stared speechlessly at his children.

"What's wrong with you both? What's the matter?" Jennifer had a sudden sense of foreboding. She sat up. "It's Beman, isn't it? Tell me, for goodness' sake."

Mrs. Meyers sighed. She reached for Jennifer's hand. "I know this won't make sense . . . I don't think any of us will ever be able to explain it." She shuddered. "Jennifer, Beman died at nine-thirty this morning, half an hour after you both left for the beach."

White Cloud

Amy lay back against her pillows. With effort, she turned her head toward the window and pulled aside the ruffled pink curtain. It was another beautiful day.

The sun gleamed down on the meadow at the back of the house. The high grass swayed gently in the breeze, and the cornflowers bowed in greeting. Along with daisies they were Amy's favorite wildflowers. It was as though they had been planted there, just for her.

She sighed and closed her eyes wearily against the sun, whose warmth could only touch her now through the window. She closed her eyes against the tall rustling grass through which she had been told she could not run.

"You can't go out, Amy," Dr. Jenkins had said sadly. "You're just too weak. I'm so sorry, my dear. Your bed is the best place for you to be."

He had brought her a beautiful book on wildflowers, but how could that make up for what she was missing in real life?

It wasn't her fault she was so ill. It wasn't anyone's fault, but that didn't make her feel any better about the way things were. She felt guilty about having had another bad night. As usual, her mother had insisted on staying with her, dozing every now and then in the easy chair by the side of the bed. She had looked so tired that morning.

Amy felt guilty about putting such a strain on her family . . . for all the sacrifices they were having to make for her sake. Her mom, giving up her part-time job, hardly ever going out, not getting enough sleep. Her dad, rushing home early from work each day, losing clients, his business suffering, yet saying nothing. Jessica, spending all her time with her, instead of with friends.

The sadness in her parents' eyes was almost too much to bear. It hurt, too, to see the tears Jessica tried so hard to hide. Jessica was only ten, just two years her junior, but she had suddenly become so grown-up and responsible since Amy had gotten so ill. It was hard to imagine now how they used to fight.

Amy felt guilty, too, for her thoughts . . . for wanting to be free of the tubes pouring liquids and medicine into her body. She wanted to be free of her dependence on the oxygen in the tank at the head of her bed . . . and free of the pain. She wanted to enjoy all the beauty denied to her outside her bedroom, which had become her prison. How she longed to be free. She knew she would be soon. Very soon.

Propped high against her four thick pillows, she peered out to see if he was there again—her beautiful friend who waited for her in the meadow. Her friend who called for her more and more frequently to join him.

How magnificent he was—pure white with a long flowing silver mane that glimmered like silk. Tall and magestic, he would toss his proud head as he whinnied for her to come. She had named him Cloud. Somehow it seemed the perfect name. He was hers, all hers. She knew that, too.

Strangely, he only came when she was alone. Nobody else had seen him. Jessica and her parents had asked about him in the town, and at the neighboring farms, but no one had seen a horse of that description.

"If I do see him, Amy, I'll take a whole roll of pictures for you," her sister had said. Jessica had searched the woods and hunted for tracks by the stream near the meadow, but there had been no trace of him.

"Jessica," her mother had said gently, "he's a figment of Amy's imagination. It's so lonely for her shut away in her room twenty-four hours a day. It must seem like a prison to her at times. With her vivid imagination, her constant fevers, and all the medicine she's taking, she only thinks she sees him. He exists only in her mind."

Jessica slipped the marker between the pages and closed the book quietly, as Amy's eyelids began to flutter shut. She could finish the chapter tomorrow. It would soon be time for another trip to the library. She had almost finished reading *The Black Stallion* to her sister.

Amy, the book-lover, who, her mother used to tease, "devoured" books, had been far too tired lately to read to herself. Each night Jessica would perch on the edge of Amy's bed and read to her. It often helped put her to sleep. Jessica felt frustrated and helpless, seeing Amy so frail and ill. At least reading to her was one of the few things she could do to make her sister feel better.

As Jessica pushed herself up from the bed a small hand reached out to touch hers. "Jess, don't be sad. Please. I'm going to be free. I'm not afraid," whispered Amy.

"Cloud's waiting for me. We'll ride through the meadow and follow the stream through Morley's Woods, and he'll take me clear to the top of Twin Peaks. I'll pick bunches of cornflowers and daisies on the way.

"I've always wanted to go to the top of Twin Peaks, but I've never been strong enough for the climb. I've looked at it through my window every day . . . out of reach, until now. Cloud and I will go there soon."

Amy slumped back breathlessly. She gently pushed away the oxygen mask Jessica tried to place over her mouth and nose. With a lump in her throat, Jessica leaned over and planted a kiss on her sister's forehead.

She stared down at Amy through misted eyes. How pale she looked. How cold she felt, yet despite that, with her long blond hair fanned out around her head like a halo, she looked the most serene . . . the most beautiful she had ever seen her.

"I love you, Amy," she whispered.

"I love you too, Jess, and Mom and Dad," came a faint reply. "Don't be sad. I just want to be free."

Those were the last words Amy was heard to speak.

Six long, heartbreaking weeks had passed since Amy had been granted her wish. Jessica and her parents grieved for themselves, but not for Amy.

"I don't think Amy would want us to

mourn forever, Jessica," said her mother. "Is there anything you'd like to do this weekend? Is there anywhere you'd like to go?" she asked. "It's been such a long time since we've really gone anywhere."

Jessica stared thoughtfully at her parents across the breakfast table. "If it's not too painful for you both . . . if it's not too soon, I'd like to go to the top of Twin Peaks. Amy wanted to go there so badly," she said.

Tears welled in her mother's eyes. "When she was little, Amy could never understand why we dared not take her . . . that we were always so afraid she'd have trouble breathing so high up on the mountain. I wish now I'd taken the risk," she added sadly. "I wish I'd taken her there, just once."

A comforting hand slipped over hers. Jessica's father cleared his throat and said, "No regrets, Meg. Amy wouldn't want that. We loved her and did our best. She knew that."

He looked over at Jessica. "Of course we'll go, Jess. We'll leave early on Saturday morning."

"Amy was so convinced Cloud would take her there. I want to see if I can find any trace of a horse up there," said Jessica.

"Jessica," chided her mother gently, "I told you. Amy's horse doesn't exist."

"I need to know that for myself, Mom," replied Jessica. "I just want to find out for myself. If he does, then I'll know Amy's happy."

Little was said on the two-hour drive to Twin Peaks Mountain. Jessica and her parents were each busy with their own thoughts, dealing with their memories and feelings in their own way.

Mr. Miller parked the station wagon at the scenic lookout point. The family got out, took their jackets from the backseat, and began the long steep trek up the mountain trail. Only the sounds of their labored breathing disturbed the quiet peace as they passed the bushes of wild elderberries and blackberries, climbing higher and higher until the mountainside became more rocky and rugged. At long last they reached the peak.

Mrs. Miller wearily sat down on a large boulder, trying to catch her breath. Jessica's father, hands on hips, stood panting, taking in the view. Fields and rolling meadows stretched as far as he could see.

Jessica did not stop to rest or admire the view. She had climbed there for a purpose. Eyes lowered, she searched for clues on the ground . . . for proof of the existence of Amy's horse.

A splash of blue, out of place on the rugged mountaintop, suddenly caught her gaze, and she hurried over to the pile of rocks where it lay. Jessica stopped abruptly and gasped in disbelief. Hardly daring to take her eyes off it, in case it should disappear, she knelt down. Dazed, she touched it. It was real! It had been tucked between two rocks. Gently she pulled it free.

"What is it, Jess? What have you found?" a voice above her asked quietly. Her father placed a hand on her shoulder.

"Look, Dad," Jessica said in awe, holding out the bunch of flowers tied with a ribbon of pink lace. "Amy's favorite wildflowers. She said she'd pick some on her way up here. Dad, I'd know this ribbon anywhere. It's Amy's. I just know it is."

Her father lifted her gently to her feet and placed a comforting arm around her shoulders. "It's a coincidence, Jess, a mere coincidence. Miracles like that don't happen." He added wistfully, "I wish they did, but what you're hoping for just isn't possible. Some other young girl picked these flowers when they were in bloom, came up here, and forgot them. That's what happened," he explained.

Before she had a chance to answer . . . to tell him that he was wrong . . . that a miracle had happened, a sudden gust of wind took them both by surprise. A large shadow cast itself in front of them, and they looked up in alarm.

Frightened, Jessica clutched her father's hand. "How can a cloud cast a shadow like this, Dad?" she asked.

"I don't know, Jess, I don't . . .".

His voice trailed off in mid-sentence as his wife grabbed hold of his arm, startling him. Her voice trembled as she said, "Look at the cloud, Jim. Just look at it." She held on to him for support as they all stared in awe at the cottony white cloud hovering above them.

The cloud had taken on an unbelievable shape—that of a young girl on a horse. Her long hair blew carelessly in the wind. The horse's mane floated in the air like strands of silk.

A sound, faint, yet definite, drifted down to the mountain peak. Jessica and her mother and father huddled together, arms wrapped around each other, united in wonder. They had all heard the same thing. Were their ears playing tricks on them, or had they really heard the sound of a horse whinnying in the wind?

Through blurry eyes Jessica stared up at the cloud and yelled, "I love you, Amy. You were right. Cloud is beautiful. Now I won't be sad for you anymore."

Captain
Fenchurch

"Well, look lively, you landlubbers. Don't just stand there. Either enter my cabin or go away." The loud gruff voice startled Susan and Peter. Susan peered nervously over her brother's shoulder at the man in the captain's cabin.

"Well, what's it to be?" he boomed. "Make up your minds, though I never did agree with having a woman on board. It's bad luck, you know. Believe me, I know all about bad luck." The twins stared in awe at the impressive figure seated at the end of a long heavy table.

A large man with a short, pointed beard and thick, curly brown hair sat at the far side of the cabin. He was dressed in an elegant old-fashioned English costume. His black jacket had a high ruffled lace collar, and his long puffed sleeves were gathered in tight cuffs. They could see the handle of his sword at his side. Draped behind him on a narrow bench was a heavily embroidered black-and-gold cape. His deep, blue eyes stared at them from under his thick, dark brows.

"Gosh!" exclaimed Peter. "Are you part of the crew? The costume of the man showing us around is nowhere near as grand as yours. At least, he was showing us around until we lost him."

"I'm not just part of the crew, lad. I'm the captain, and I'm dressed as befits a true gentleman. This is my cabin. Are you coming in or not?" he asked.

Susan glanced at her brother. They were on a field trip with their sixth-grade class to explore and learn about *The Mariner,* a replica of a sixteenth-century sailing ship. Their curiosity and chattering had caused them to become separated from their classmates. They knew they should join them, or they'd be in trouble with Ms. Scott, their teacher. Still, the man looked very interesting.

"Must be all right, Susan," Peter said, "or he'd have sent us off to join the others."

Susan followed her brother into the cabin. "Look, Susan," Peter whispered excitedly, "he's dressed up to look like the man in the picture."

"Dressed up! What do you mean, dressed up!" the man exclaimed. "I am not dressed up. The man in the painting is me. Captain Richard Fenchurch at your service!"

The twins looked at each other, puzzled. Was someone playing a joke on them? "Fenchurch?" asked Peter in astonishment. "Did you say Fenchurch? How do you spell it?"

"F-E-N-C-H-U-R-C-H. I must say, you seem very interested in my name, lad," he replied.

The man beckoned for them to sit on the narrow bench near him. There were no other chairs at the table, except for the one he was sitting on. "That's our name, Fenchurch. I'm Peter, and this is my twin sister, Susan," explained Peter.

"Our great-grandfather came from

England," Peter informed the man as he settled himself down on the bench, "from a city called Norwich, in the county of Norfolk."

"Why, bless my soul, though it's a bit late for that now, that's where I hail from, Norwich, Norfolk. Perhaps that explains it," exclaimed the captain.

"Explains what?" asked Peter. "What does it explain?"

"Why, lad, the very fact that we're talking to each other right now. I don't show myself to too many people, you know. I'm always on board but rarely seen. People know I'm around, though." The mere mention of that, for some reason, had him chuckling.

"I reckon we must be kinfolk from the House of Fenchurch in Norwich . . . an amazing coincidence," said Captain Fenchurch. He leaned forward and stared intently at Peter. "Why, you even have curly brown hair like mine."

"It is a possibility, isn't it?" said Susan excitedly. "For as far back as we know, someone in our family has been connected with the sea. Our grandfather was in the navy, and our dad is a naval commander at Mare Island Naval Base. He's in charge of a nuclear submarine. I can't wait to tell him we might have met a relative from England.

"Maybe you could even come and visit us while you're in America. And perhaps, one day, we could visit you in England. It'd be really interesting to meet some of our English relatives," said Susan.

"That won't be possible, I'm afraid, lass. I haven't set foot on land for centuries. I can't leave this ship. Now, pray tell me, what is a submarine?" Captain Fenchurch asked.

Peter chuckled. He winked at Susan. This tour guide was good. He played his part well. Peter decided to play along with his game.

"It's a ship that moves underwater," he said.

The cabin shook with the man's hearty laughter. "Always liked someone with a good sense of humor . . . underwater ship indeed . . . a ship that sails underwater!" he said.

Peter, entering into the spirit of the game, said, "Oh, no. It doesn't sail. A submarine is powered by engines."

The man slapped his side as he laughed. "Submarines . . . engines? What are you? Jesters? Inventors of new words? Queen Elizabeth would love having you at court. She would find you most amusing . . . and reward you most handsomely, I daresay."

Susan smiled as she kicked Peter in the shins. "That'd be Queen Elizabeth the Second, right?"

The man frowned. "Don't be absurd. There's never been an Elizabeth on the throne before her. There's only one Queen Elizabeth."

Susan and Peter chuckled. The guide was a very good actor. They hadn't caught him on a single mistake yet.

"Are you a pirate?" Peter asked.

"Bless my soul! Oh, dear, there I go again. No. I'm not a pirate. I sail the seas, attacking and plundering enemy ships with the blessing of the queen herself. I'm a privateer and proud of it. I give all the treasures I take to my queen, who rewards me handsomely. There's a great difference, you know, between a common pirate and a privateer," explained Captain Fenchurch.

"Who exactly is the enemy?" Susan asked.

"Why, the Spaniards, of course." His eyes took on a distant look. "Why, there are so many battles I could tell you about. . . ."

His voice trailed off as he reached into a pocket in his jacket. "Here. Take this as a token of my pleasure at meeting you today." He tossed something at Peter that gleamed in the sunlight shining through the cabin window. Peter caught the object deftly in his right hand. His eyes opened wide in amazement.

"Wow, Susan! Look at this. It even looks real," exclaimed Peter.

Captain Fenchurch looked puzzled. "Of course it's real. It's a silver coin, part of a treasure chest plundered from a Spanish ship. Keep it."

Peter stared down at the coin. It looked valuable. Why would the guide be giving him something like that? He almost hoped it was fake, otherwise he'd have a lot of explaining to do. Suddenly he had an idea. He'd bring Ms. Scott to the cabin to meet the man calling himself Captain Fenchurch. That would make everything all right.

"Ms. Scott!" Peter gasped.

Amy looked at him in alarm. "What's the matter, Peter?" she asked.

"I was so fascinated by Captain Fenchurch that I forgot about our class. Remember, Ms. Scott told us to stay together as a group . . . or else!" he said.

"Just a few more minutes, Peter. Perhaps Captain Fenchurch can help with our assignments," said Susan.

Susan looked hopefully at the man. "Tomorrow we have to write a short essay about the trip, with at least ten facts we've learned. Would you give us some information?" she asked.

"I know every piece of timber and every single cabin like the back of my hand. I can tell you anything there is to be told about this old ship.

"'Twas built in Plymouth, England, in

1570 . . . at least building started that year. It took almost two years to build. Months were spent seeking trees with trunks large enough to make up the vessel's ribs. The timbers used are mainly oak, elm, and pine. Its overall length is one hundred feet, and its weight is one hundred tons. How am I doing so far?" asked Captain Fenchurch.

"Great," Susan and Peter said in unison as they scribbled furiously in their small notepads.

"Thanks. This is wonderful," Amy added. "Will you tell us more?"

Captain Fenchurch seemed more than happy to continue. "This is my cabin . . . the Great Cabin. I have eighty crewmen. Forty must stay in readiness on the deck. The men take turns either sleeping there or in the forecastle. It's a tough life. . . ."

His voice trailed off as he was interrupted by a loud anxious voice outside the cabin.

"Amy! Peter! Answer me!" yelled Ms. Scott.

Susan stopped writing and groaned. "It's our teacher. She sounds angry." She and

Peter jumped up and rushed past the astonished Captain Fenchurch. Susan turned in the doorway. "Please tell her we've been here with your permission, or we're in a lot of trouble."

"There you are," bellowed an angry voice. "I've searched high and low for you both. Weren't you told to stay with your group? I am very angry."

An irate Ms. Scott towered in front of them. She stood with her feet apart, her hands on her hips. Her face was flushed. They had never seen her look so angry.

Susan glanced at her watch. She suddenly realized they'd been missing for at least fifteen or twenty minutes. They were the teacher's responsibility. They could have fallen overboard . . . or anything. "I'm really sorry, Ms. Scott," she said apologetically.

"So am I, Ms. Scott," said Peter. "We were so engrossed in talking with Captain Fenchurch—at least, that's who he says he is—that we lost track of time."

"Come and talk to him. He'll tell you he invited us into his cabin. He might well be a distant relative of ours from England," explained Susan.

Ms. Scott made a noise that sounded like a snort. She glared at them and marched past them into the cabin. They sheepishly followed behind. Susan gasped. Peter shook his head. Captain Fenchurch, and all traces of him, had disappeared.

"How did he get by us?" Susan whispered. "Now she'll never believe us."

"So. You were talking to a Captain Fenchurch, were you?" thundered Ms. Scott. "Where is he? Is he a magician with magical powers to disappear into thin air? I must say, I'm amazed at your lack of imagination. You could have made up a more convincing name.

"Disobeying my instructions is bad enough, but to tell me a blatant lie on top of that is intolerable. I shall call your parents when we return to school. I'll recommend you be banned from further field trips for the rest of the school year. I'm surprised and disappointed in you both. Captain Fenchurch indeed!" ranted Ms. Scott.

"We're telling the truth," Susan said

miserably. "Captain Fenchurch, where are you? Can't you see we're in trouble? Please come back and let our teacher know you're real," she pleaded.

Suddenly Ms. Scott gasped. The twins followed the direction of her astonished gaze. A chess piece, carved from wood into the head of a soldier, was moving slowly across the chessboard. In an instant it stopped.

"L-look a-at the p-painting!" stammered Susan in disbelief. The picture had turned itself around to face the wall.

"Look at that pewter mug!" Peter exclaimed in awe as it sailed through the air past Ms. Scott's nose, just as she slumped down onto the bench.

"Are you okay, Ms. Scott?" he asked in alarm. The teacher's face had gone pale. Her hands were trembling. She slowly shook her head.

"Since, as far as I know, neither of you are magicians, I shall assume you are not responsible for what we have just witnessed. This is one of the strangest experiences of my life. Let's find the tour guide to see what he has to say. Help me up, would you? My legs feel rather wobbly," said Ms. Scott.

They found the guide and the rest of the class up on deck. The young man, dressed as an old English sailor in a pair of beige pants, white shirt, and a red cap, looked up in relief. "Ah. You found them. I was beginning to worry." He laughed as he added, "I thought they might have bumped into Captain Fenchurch. I was saving his story until you got back here."

Susan gasped, Peter looked stunned, and Ms. Scott's face paled even further. She had to sit down. "What's the matter?" the guide asked in alarm. "What's wrong?"

In a less than steady voice Ms. Scott answered, "They said they'd been talking to Captain Fenchurch in his cabin. He told them they might be related.

"I didn't believe them, as I never saw him, but things . . . eerie things happened in the cabin. I would never have believed it had I not seen for myself. Things began to move around on their own. What's the explanation? Who's Captain Fenchurch?" she asked.

The guide was no longer laughing. His eyes were opened wide in astonishment. He was quiet for a while. The children were silent, waiting expectantly.

"Richard Fenchurch was captain of the original ship over four hundred years ago. It's his portrait that hangs in the captain's cabin. Some say he's still on board, causing strange things to happen.

"A skeleton crew—sorry, perhaps that's not the best choice of words—sleeps on board now. They've reported that strange things happen at night ... things move around or disappear. It's said that Captain Richard Fenchurch is doomed to walk the decks of this ship forever. His spirit can't find rest. I'll tell you the story. That's all I can do, because I can't explain what happened to you or the peculiar things that happen on this ship."

The guide had a captive audience. There was no fidgeting or talking.

"Richard Fenchurch came from a wealthy family in England. He didn't want to be a rich landowner like his father, so he ran away to sea when he was a young boy of twelve." The guide glanced at Peter. "He would have been about your age. His father disowned him. He would never again accept him as his son.

"An elderly sea captain took a liking to the boy, took him on board his ship, and taught him everything he knew. They became pirates, plundering Spanish ships. Both of them became very wealthy. When the old captain died, he left Richard Fenchurch his ship.

"Soon Captain Fenchurch's exploits came to the attention of Queen Elizabeth. She didn't like people stealing treasures and keeping them for themselves. She had Richard Fenchurch captured and brought before her at court.

"He impressed her greatly. She realized he was no ordinary pirate. She asked him to plunder Spanish ships for her. The treasures were needed to pay for ships to be built that could defeat the ships of England's enemy, Spain. He agreed—he really had no choice —and became a privateer.

"He was very successful, and the queen rewarded him well. She was able to build more ships, and in 1570 Richard Fenchurch had enough money to have a ship of his own built. In 1573 he set sail in his new ship, *The Norfolk,* as Sir Richard Fenchurch. He was knighted by the queen, on the very spot I'm sitting.

"It was said that Captain Fenchurch was a kind and fair man. He rewarded his men well for defeating the Spanish in battle, and taking their gold and jewels for the queen of England. But then the men became greedy.

"In December of 1580, after a particularly profitable battle, *The Norfolk* was almost keeling over from the weight of all the captured treasure. The temptation proved too strong for the men. There was a mutiny."

There were gasps of dismay as the guide said, "Captain Fenchurch was tied to the main mast and shot. All other officers and men loyal to him were shot and thrown overboard. The captain's dead body followed soon after.

"Sailors are very superstitious. It was bad luck for a life to be taken on board ship by a fellow crewman's hand. Superstition demanded the ship's name be changed. The old figurehead was hacked off, and the ship's carpenters were summoned to make a new figurehead. The ship was renamed *The Mariner.*

"The men were now outlaws. They knew they could never return to England. They had learned of the existence of distant lands from Sir Francis Drake's epic voyage, and they set sail in search of them. Unfortunately for them, the mutineers made two big mistakes.

"First of all, fearing the wrath of God, they dared not shoot the ship's chaplain, a religious man. They merely tossed him overboard. He managed to cling to a piece of wreckage and was rescued by a British sailing ship. He was taken back to England to tell the story. Without him, it would have been believed that the ship had been lost at sea.

"Furious that the mutineers had not only stolen from her, but had also killed her favorite privateer, Queen Elizabeth sent out ships to hunt them down.

"Finally the ship was recognized, despite its new figurehead, and after a short battle the ship was captured. The mutineers that survived received the standard punishment for striking an officer. They had one of their hands nailed to the main mast and chopped off."

There were shudders of horror from the fascinated listeners. "You must realize that you can't work on a sailing ship with only one hand," continued the guide. "You need one to work with and one to hold on with." He pointed up to the rigging. "Can you imagine climbing up there to look for enemy ships with only one hand?

"The mutineers were forced to sail the ship back to England. Quite a few fell overboard by the time the ship reached shore. It was said that some had a helping hand over the side. Strange things had begun to happen. It was then that the mutineers realized their second big mistake. When Captain Fenchurch's body was tossed overboard, they forgot to bless his soul. His spirit was doomed to haunt the ship forever."

There was a buzz of excited chatter. Susan said excitedly, "That's what Captain Fenchurch kept saying, 'Bless my soul.' He's real. I know it." She held out her notepad for the guide to see. "Look at the facts he gave us about the ship."

"And this is real enough, isn't it?" said Peter, holding out the coin. "Poor Captain Fenchurch."

Peter suddenly had an idea. "Captain Fenchurch," he called out, "if you don't want to walk these decks forever, give me a sign. Make something happen. I have a plan."

For a moment it seemed as though nothing were about to happen. "Look at that bucket," whispered one of the students in disbelief as it floated in the air.

"Check out that rope!" yelled Susan. A

sturdy coil of rope, curled tight like a sleeping snake, was rapidly unwinding itself.

Suddenly everything was still. Everyone had the secret hope that something else would happen. They also had the secret fear of what it might be.

"Captain Fenchurch!" Peter yelled. "Tonight the entire Fenchurch family of Benicia, California, is going to do something the mutineers and the Fenchurch family in England should have done in 1580. We're all going to church to pray for your soul."

As the excited, chattering fifth-graders climbed down the ramp to the dock, wondering if anyone would believe what had happened on their field trip, Susan and Peter held back. A strong hand clamped itself over Peter's shoulder. "Would you really do that for me, lad?" asked the familiar voice.

"It's the least we Fenchurches can do," Susan said, impulsively planting a kiss on his cheek. "We'll come back every day that the ship's here to make sure you've really gone."

Peter held out his hand. He shook the icy-cold hand of the man who had been dead for over four hundred years. "Good-bye, Captain. Rest in peace," he said.

With tears in his eyes, Richard Fenchurch said with surprising gentleness, "Fare thee well, Susan and Peter Fenchurch of Benicia. 'Twas a glad day for me when you came aboard my ship."

From where she stood on the dock, Ms. Scott could see the twins talking to someone, but she couldn't see who. She watched as they turned and waved. The tour guide had left with them. As far as she knew, there was no one else on board. Who was she, though, to question things she did not understand? This was the day sane, sensible Cecilia Scott found herself believing in ghosts.